POOH AND PIGL
GO HUNTIN(

Pooh wasn't quite sure whose footprints he and Piglet were following. He thought it might be the Woozles, or other Hostile Animals. They were quite relieved to discover Tigger and Roo. Tigger had bounced himself into trouble again, and was delighted when Christopher Robin arrived to rescue him.

Other titles in this series:

POOH AND THE HONEY TREE
WINNIE-THE-POOH AND THE BLUSTERY DAY
POOH IN A TIGHT PLACE
WINNIE-THE-POOH AND TIGGER TOO

Scholastic Book Services Inc.,
10 Earlham Street, London WC2N 9LN

Scholastic Inc.,
730 Broadway, New York, NY 10003, USA

Scholastic Tab Publications Ltd.,
123 Newkirk Road, Richmond Hill,
Ontario L4C 3G5, Canada

Ashton Scholastic Pty. Ltd., Box 579, Gosford,
New South Wales, Australia

Ashton Scholastic Ltd., 165 Marua Road,
Panmure, Auckland, New Zealand

First published in West Germany by Ravensburger Taschenbücher, 1983
First published in the UK by Scholastic Book Services Inc., 1985
Illustrations copyright © Walt Disney, 1983
This translation copyright © Scholastic Book Services, 1985
Translated by Anthea Bell
Original title *Spuren im Schnee*
ISBN 0 590 70412 5

Made and printed in Spain by
Printer industria gráfica s.a. Barcelona
D.L.B. 2933-1985

POOH AND PIGLET GO HUNTING

Translated by Anthea Bell

Hippo Books
Scholastic Book Services
London

Dear Old Pooh Bear

Pooh and I first met over fifty years ago.
We used to share a room. What I mean is, Pooh
and his friends lived with me.
Grown-ups used to say Pooh and Piglet, Tigger
and Rabbit, and Kanga and Roo were only
stuffed toy animals. But that's not true! We all
lived in a wonderful world of make-believe called
the Hundred Acre Wood. And of course it was a
real Hundred Acre Wood, and it stood in the
middle of a real Forest.
"Hallo, Christopher Robin!" said Pooh.
"Hallo, Pooh Bear," I said. "Come on, we must
go on with your story! Shall we tell the story
about the Woozles?"
"No, not that one, Christopher Robin," growled
Pooh.
"All right, then I'll tell the story about Tigger,
and how he tried to climb a tree."
"Not that one either, Christopher Robin!" said
Pooh. "Can't you think of a *nice* story? A story
about Me, for instance."

Winnie-the-Pooh is a dear old Bear, and you can call him Winnie-the-Pooh, or Pooh Bear, or just plain Pooh. He likes all his names. And *of course* he likes stories about Pooh.

He thinks Pooh-stories are the best stories in the world. . .

We all lived in the Forest. Pooh had just one little weakness: he was very fond of honey. He loved eating honey. He had eaten so much he was getting quite fat. He had a song about honey.

"Isn't it funny
How a bear likes honey?
Buzz! Buzz! Buzz!
I wonder why he does?"

And he had another song he used to sing, about himself.

"Winnie-the-Pooh, Winnie-the-Pooh!
Tubby little cubby all stuffed with fluff!
I'm Winnie-the-Pooh, Winnie-the-Pooh!
Willy-nilly silly old Bear!"

Winter in the Forest

Deep snow had fallen in the Forest.
Baby Roo was waiting for Tigger to come and play.
"When's Tigger coming?" asked Roo impatiently. "I want to go out and play!"
"He'll soon be here, Roo dear," said Kanga soothingly.
Kanga was Roo's mother.
At last Tigger came bouncing through the snow.
"Hallooo, Roo! Here I am! Isn't that a nice surprise?"
"Yes! I like surprises!" said Roo happily. He was always full of high spirits.
"Hallo, Kanga!" said Tigger, bouncing.
"Hallo, Tigger!" said Kanga.
"Want to come out bouncing with me, little Roo?" asked Tigger.
"Yes, yes! We're best of all the animals at bouncing, aren't we?" said Roo.

"Now just a moment, Roo," said Kanga. "Keep still, dear. You can go bouncing in a minute." She was trying to tie a scarf round Roo's neck.

"I'll get all warm with bouncing," said Roo.

"Yes dear, and mind you don't lose your scarf," said Kanga.

"Not so tight!" said Roo.

"There! Sure you've got enough warm clothes on?" asked Kanga.

"Yes!" said Roo, impatient to be off.

Tigger was looking forward to going bouncing. Bouncing was what he did best of all. "Ready yet, Roo?" he asked. "Come on!"

"And mind you're back in time for lunch!" Kanga told them both. "Roo will need his afternoon rest. Now, do be careful!"

"We will, don't you worry!" said Tigger. "I'll keep my eye on little Roo!"

And they went off through the snow.

There was a little lake in the Hundred Acre Wood. It was frozen into hard, smooth ice now. Rabbit was skating on the surface. "What a lovely day!" said Rabbit to himself, happily. "Peace and quiet! And no Tigger anywhere in sight!"

Rabbit did not get on very well with Tigger, because Tigger was always bouncing at him. But Tigger and Baby Roo got on very well indeed.

"Look, Roo!" said Tigger. "There's old Long Ears!"

"Can Tiggers skate too?" asked Roo. "Can they skate as well as Rabbits?"

"*Can* Tiggers skate? Skating is what Tiggers do best of all!" said Tigger, and he took a run and jumped on the ice. . .

. . .and next moment his legs were slipping and sliding on the smooth ice, going in all directions. "Help!" shouted Tigger. "Watch out, Long Ears!"

"Can't you go sliding somewhere else?" said Rabbit crossly.

"W-will you show me how to do it?" quavered Tigger.

"Why won't anyone leave me alone?" snapped Rabbit, skating away. "*I* don't go bothering other people, do I?"

Tigger slid over to the bank and landed in a big pile of snow. He disappeared from sight.

"Oh, Tigger, are you all right?" shouted Roo.

Tigger emerged from the snow. "Brrr!" he said, shaking himself. "Tiggers don't think much of skating. They can *do* it all right, they're very good at it, but they just don't happen to like it!"

And Tigger and Roo went off bouncing and jumping into the Forest, looking for more games to play.

Pooh and Piglet go Hunting

While Tigger and Roo were sliding on the pond

Pooh and Piglet were trudging through the snowy Forest on their short little legs. It was cold, and the winter sunlight made the Hundred Acre Wood look strange and different.

Pooh was staring down at some tracks in the snow, wondering about them. He thought and thought and thought. . .

"Are you looking for something, Pooh?" asked Piglet. His squeaky voice didn't sound very brave.

"Ssh, Piglet!" said Pooh. "I'm tracking something."

"Tracking what?"

"That's just what I'm asking myself. What, I ask myself?"

"And what do you think you'll answer?" asked Piglet.

"I shall have to wait till I get to the end of the track," said Pooh. "Then I'll find out."

"Pooh," said Piglet, admiringly, "you really are very clever, for a Bear of Very Little Brain!"

"Thank you, Piglet," said Pooh, and suddenly he added, "Aha!"

"Aha what? Is it the track?" asked Piglet. His

voice was shaking a bit.

"This is very mysterious Piglet. There are *two* sets of tracks now!"

Pooh was right! They had come to a place where the tracks met, and crossed, but he could see two

different sets of paw marks, quite clearly.
"Piglet, whatever these tracks belong to, they
make me feel a bit peculiar," said Pooh. "All the
tracks are leading in our direction!" His voice
was husky, and he shook his head thoughtfully.

"They might," he added, "be made by Woozles!
I only hope we don't meet any Woozles, Piglet!"
"Woozles?" asked Piglet, feeling frightened.
"Pooh, are–are Woozles Hostile Animals?"
"They may be," said Pooh, mysteriously, "and
then again, they may not. You never can tell,

with Woozles. I *hope* not!"

"So . . . so do I!" said Piglet.

Pooh and Piglet went on, feeling rather scared in
case the tracks led straight to Woozles, and the
Woozles turned out to be hostile.

Neither of them realized that they were going
round in circles, and it was their *own* paw marks
they were looking at.

"Woozles!" said Piglet again. "Oh dear! These
tracks look very new too, don't they?"

Pooh decided to make up an Outdoor Song
which had to be sung in the snow, to cheer them
up, so he made it up and sang it to Piglet. It
went:

"The more it snows
(Tiddely pom),
The more it goes
(Tiddely pom),
The more it goes
(Tiddely pom),
On snowing.
And nobody knows
(Tiddely pom),

How cold my toes
(Tiddely pom),
How cold my toes
(Tiddely pom),
Are growing."

Then they both sang it, with Piglet putting in the
tiddely-poms and Pooh doing the rest of it, and
they felt a bit better.

All of a sudden they heard a loud voice. "Help!"

"Oh dear!" said Piglet in alarm. "I wonder what
that is?"

"Hallooo!" came the voice again. "Help!"

"Piglet, look!" said Pooh. "There's something in
that tree!"

"Is it one of the Fiercer Animals, do you think?"
asked Piglet. "Is it a Woozle?"

"Help! Help!" said the strange voice again.

"It sounds more like a Jagular," said Pooh.

"What. . .what do Jagulars do?" asked Piglet.

"They shout, 'Help! Help!' and when you look
up they drop on you."

"I'm looking *down!*" called Piglet. His knees
were shaking.

More About Tigger

But now I can tell you what else happened to
Tigger and little Roo in the the snow in the
Forest!
"Can Tiggers climb trees?" asked Roo.
"Climbing trees is what they do best of all!" said
Tigger. "They're up and down trees all day!
Only they don't *climb* trees, they *bounce* up trees!
I'll show you! Come on! That was a good
bounce, eh?"
And Tigger went shooting up the tree.
Now he was right at the top of it, and when he
looked down for the first time he felt quite dizzy.
"I didn't know this was such a *tall* tree. . ." he
said.

Roo was holding on to Tigger's tail. Tigger
didn't like being so high above the ground.
"Oo, Tigger, oo, Tigger, what fun!" squeaked
Roo, swinging excitedly from the end of Tigger's
tail.
"Stop it!" said Tigger. "Don't *do* that, Roo!"
By now Tigger was feeling very frightened
indeed.
"All right," said Roo, and he took a jump and
landed on a branch.
Thank goodness, thought Tigger. I feel quite ill,
with this tree shaking in the wind!

Tigger was feeling worse and worse. He was
terrified, in fact. There he was at the top of the
tree, and he didn't know how to get down again!
Now what?

Tigger clung tightly to a branch and shouted,
"Help! Help!" And then he shouted "Halloo!"
And then he shouted "Help!" again.

And that was when Pooh and Piglet began to be
afraid of meeting a Woozle, or a Jagular, or one
of the other Fiercer Animals. . .

Not a Woozle and Not a Jagular

"Look, Tigger!" squeaked Roo. "Here come Pooh and Piglet!"

"Hallo!" growled Pooh. "It's Roo and Tigger, not a Woozle or a Jagular at all!"

"Hallo, Roo!" called Piglet. "What are you two doing up that tree?"

"Nothing much," said Roo happily. "Tigger's stuck, and we can't get down! What fun! We'll have to stay here for ever!"

"I need help!" groaned Tigger. "I need help *fast!* Fetch Christopher Robin!"

As soon as Christopher Robin and the rest of his friends knew Tigger needed help, they all came hurrying up to the tree.

"Now then, what's the matter, Pooh?" asked Christopher Robin.

"Tigger and Roo are stuck," said Pooh.

"Oh dear!" cried Kanga. "Oh, Roo, however did you get up there?"

"We bounced up!" said Roo, proudly.

"Oh, do be careful, dear!"

"I'm all right!" said Roo. "But I'm a bit worried

about Tigger!"

"Serves him right!" said Rabbit. "Now he can't bounce at any of us!"

"But we've got to get him down!" said Pooh and Piglet.

Rabbit wasn't sure that he agreed.

Christopher Robin took off his jacket. "Come on, all of you! If we each hold a corner they can jump down. You jump first, Roo!"

They held the jacket out, and Roo took off and jumped, right into the middle of it.

"Oo, lovely!" said Roo. "Oo, what fun! Come on, Tigger, it doesn't hurt! Come on, jump!"

"Tiggers don't jump," said Tigger. "Tiggers bounce!"

"Well, bounce, then!" said Baby Roo.

"Tiggers don't bounce *down* trees," said Tigger. "They only bounce *up* them."

Tigger didn't want to jump down, or bounce down, or climb down.

"Good. He'll have to stay up that tree for ever!" said Rabbit.

"For ever? Oh no! I promise I'll never, never bounce any of you again if only I get down

safely!" moaned poor Tigger.

"Never, never?" said Rabbit. "Well, mind you don't forget! You promised! Did everybody hear him?"

Then everyone tried persuading Tigger to come down. He wailed and made such a fuss that in the end Christopher Robin simply went and took him out of the tree, and put him down on the ground.

"There you are," he said. "You're safe now, Tigger!"

"Oh my goodness! Oh, I'm so glad to be down!" cried Tigger. "I'm so glad to be down I could bounce at you all for joy!"

"Oh no, you couldn't! You promised!" said Rabbit.

"Promised what?" asked Tigger. "Oh–you mean I mustn't bounce anyone any more?"

"Never, never again!" said Rabbit.

"Not even a teeny, tiny little bounce?" said Tigger, sounding dreadfully sad.

"Not even a teeny, tiny little bounce!" said Rabbit sternly.

"Poor Tigger!" said Pooh. "I feel so sorry for him!"

"Christopher Robin, I liked the old Tigger best, when he *could* bounce!" said Piglet.

"So did I!" said everyone else except Rabbit.

"What about you, Rabbit?" asked Christopher Robin.

"Oh, all right, all right!" said Rabbit. "*I* liked the old Tigger best too."

"Oh, Rabbit!" said Tigger. "You mean I can

bounce again, the way I did before?"
And he took hold of Rabbit, swung him through
the air and cried, "Come on, Long Ears, let's
both bounce together!"
"You mean you want *me* to bounce?" said
Rabbit, in some alarm.

"Yes, of course! Come on! Your legs are just made for bouncing! It feels like flying!"
And when Rabbit tried it, he found he really did enjoy bouncing!
Soon they were all jumping and bouncing and running, and having a lovely time.

It had been a really exciting winter's day in the Forest. All the animals went home to Christopher Robin's house, and he lit a nice warm fire. They had a lovely evening playing games.

Pooh had a nice evening too. He had missed his elevenses. He hadn't even had time for a little something. So of course he had to make up for that. And when he looked in his pots of honey, they were full.

"Thank you, Christopher Robin, thank you for all this lovely honey!" he said happily.

So that's the end of the story about Tigger and Pooh and Piglet and the Woozles.
Aren't there any such things as Woozles, then? Well, I've known Pooh ever since I was seven, and Pooh would never say anything that wasn't true. Grown-ups may say we just made up all these stories, but of course that isn't true! There are Woozles as sure as there's a Hundred Acre Wood. As sure as Heffalumps are Heffalumps, and as sure as my name is Christopher Robin!

The next book tells you more of Pooh's adventures, and you will meet some real Heffalumps. And there is a Blustery Day, and a flood. Oh, yes, and Eeyore loses his tail. But Christopher Robin – that's me – knows what to do about it.